MW01179182

Table of Contents

Chapter 1

Heather Shepherd fastened her Donut Delights apron and stepped up to the silver counter in the kitchen of her store.

Her assistants, three of them, at least – Maricela and Ken manned the counter out front, and Ames was on errands – gathered around her, elbow to elbow.

"All right," she said, "so, I've taught the others how to make this week's donut, and it's about time I teach you guys too. It's really simple, but it's a crowd pleaser."

Jung rubbed his palms together. "I can't wait."

"What is it, boss?" Angelica asked.

Emily Potts licked her lips and brushed off her apron. She'd been the quietest of the bunch since she'd joined their team.

"We've got Thanksgiving coming up," Heather said, "so I thought we'd do a pumpkin themed donut. The Iced Pumpkin donut, to be precise."

"Oh gosh, I'm getting hungry already."

"We really want this to be a little chunk of Thanksgiving with every bite." Heather smiled at them all. "Minus the turkey, of course."

Heather tapped her fingers to the side of a steel bowl. "We've got fresh roasted cinnamon pumpkin, which we'll mash up to add to the batter. Then add in some ginger for flavor, as well, and a touch of condensed milk. Flour, of course, whole grain, the best Ames can find. This is going to be quite a heavy, cake-like mixture."

"So, you'll do a light glaze then?" Emily asked. She might be quiet, but she learned super-fast.

"That's exactly right, Emily." Heather beamed at her youngest assistant and Angelica gave her a thumbs up. "I want this donut double-dipped in a very simple vanilla glaze. We'll do a tiny splash of lemon juice in the glaze, to add a little zing to each bite, but the predominant flavor is going to be the cinnamon and pumpkin."

"Wow," Jung breathed.

"It's supposed to excite the taste buds," Heather said and tickled her fingers in front of her lips. "They're cooked in the oven. Okay, so let's get started."

The assistants shuffled closer still. Emily whipped out a notepad and scratched across it with her pen.

"First off, we're going to mash up —"

The kitchen door swung inward, and Geoff Lawless stepped into the room, closely followed by Ken. "I'm sorry, Heather, I couldn't stop him," her assistant said, and frowned at the big, bald guy. "He ran past me before I could."

"That's okay, Ken," Heather said. She stepped back from the counter, and curiosity twirled through her belly. "You guys mash up the pumpkin and spice it with cinnamon. I've put the recipe on the counter. Carry on with the batter, but don't cook it until I've come back to have a taste."

"Aye, aye, captain," Jung said and saluted.

Heather rolled her eyes at him, then chuckled and walked over to Geoff Lawless.

For many weeks, the man had been a sheer pain in her neck, but that'd changed last week.

His mockery of a donut store had closed, and he'd quit his incessant Heather-stalking ways.

"Geoff?" Heather said. "Do you want to talk in my office?"

He shook his head in reply but drew her off to one side of the kitchen. It was huge, after the renovations – the others couldn't possibly hear them.

"What's going on?"

"Had to come," Geoff said. "Had to come to warn you about her."

Heather's insides turned frosty. She'd been through enough investigations and odd situations to sense another one incoming. "About who?"

Geoff glanced back at the kitchen doors and swallowed, loudly. "Kate. My sister. She's coming for you."

Heather's nerves jittered, but she kept her face smooth as red velvet donut. "What do you mean?"

"Kate's setting up another bakery. Another store to compete with you," Geoff said.

Heather arched both eyebrows. "Oh, that's not so bad."

"It's a cupcake store. She wants to set up right down the road. She's going to try to steal your customers."

"I see," Heather replied. "Thanks a lot for warning me, Geoff. I appreciate that." She patted him awkwardly on the shoulder. "But I don't think you or I need to worry about Kate Laverne. She can set up the store if she wants, but she's got a lot of work to do before she can compete with us."

Heather had all the confidence in the world in her store and her staff. They were a family, and nothing could break that.

"She's dangerous," Geoff said, darkly. "She'll do anything to get what she wants. Be careful, Shepherd. Watch your back."

"Thanks. I'll do that, Geoff." Heather walked toward the door, and he joined her. She pushed it open, and they traipsed out into the storefront of Donut Delights.

People chattered and ate donuts, and they slurped milkshakes and coffee, their coats over the backs of their chairs or hanging on hooks against one wall. The golden boards glinted beneath the downlights overhead.

Oh, yeah, it'd taken Heather ages to get her store to this point. Full every day, online orders pouring in and happy customers. If Kate thought she could compete, well, she could bring it on.

"Would you like to stay for a donut, Geoff? On the house."

Lawless' thin lips twisted to one side. "No thanks. I can't eat 'em. Not since the other place."

"I understand," Heather said. "Well, if you ever need anything, you just let me know."

"Just be careful," he repeated. "She's not right. She's not good. Be careful, Shepherd." And then he loped toward the door, in classic Geoff style, and brushed past several customers on his way.

They stared at him in consternation.

Heather couldn't help but chuckle. Somehow, she'd made the weirdest friend she'd ever had in her entire life.

Geoff pushed out into the blustery fall morning, and the bell tinkled overhead. Amy jumped out of his path and stared at him, then hurried indoors and toward the front counter.

"What was that about? Geoff up to his old tricks?"

"Nope," Heather replied. "All different ones, this time."

Chapter 2

Heather looped her arm through her bestie's and walked down the street. Lilly trotted along beside her, and Dave set their pace, his doggy claws scrabbling along the rough concrete of the sidewalk.

"Just another week in paradise," Heather sang.

"If paradise is freezing cold," Amy replied, and clutched the edge of her coat with her free hand. "This is ridiculous."

"We're in Texas, Amy," Lilly said. "It's not that bad."

"Says, you." Amy stuck out her tongue, then winked at the little girl.

"Ames has always had a low tolerance for cool weather. And the hot weather," Heather said, and tapped her chin. "Now that I think of it, you have a low tolerance for almost every kind of weather."

"It's simple, really." Amy gestured with her hand. "All I want is clear, blue skies, a moderately warm day and a hint of a breeze. Just a hint. No rain, no freezing winds, no boiling sun. Is that too much to ask?"

"Yeah," Heather and Lilly said, in unison. Dave barked his agreement.

"Always ganging up on me," Amy muttered and pursed her lips.

It was an act, of course. Heather's bestie could never stay mad at them.

They continued their journey through suburbia. Houses and gardens passed by. Some had picket fences; others had trees. A dog yapped from behind a fence and launched himself at it.

Dave ignored him and padded on. One sniff was all it took to determine how interesting the object was. The dog had failed Dave's test, for sure.

"Thanksgiving is on the way," Heather said. "Where are you going to be, Ames? With Kent?"

"No," she replied, swiftly, then looked at the top of Lilly's head. "I, uh, I hoped to spend Thanksgiving with you guys, if that's okay?"

"Of course. I kinda hoped you'd say that." Heather patted her bestie's arm and smiled.

A scream pierced the late afternoon air. This time, Dave barked, loudly. Lilly froze in her tracks, and Amy pulled up short, too.

"What on earth?" Heather let go of her bestie and hurried forward. "What was that?"

"A sign to turn back?" Amy suggested.

Lilly grasped her hand. "I don't like this."

The scream rang out again, from a house two doors down. Heather pressed her lips together, then fished her phone out of her pocket. She'd already assigned Ryan's office number to speed dial.

Heather looked back at her favorite folks. "Amy, please will you take Lilly and Dave home."

"Au-Heather. It's dangerous. You should come too," Lilly whispered.

"No, sweetie. I'll be fine. Amy will stay with you until I'm back. Right, Ames?"

"Of course," Amy said, then turned and led Lilly away.

"Mom," Lilly called.

"I'll be home, soon. I promise, Lils," Heather said, and her heart skipped a beat. Whenever Lilly let the 'm' word slip, that happened.

Heather pressed the button and dialed Ryan's number. She pressed the phone to her ear and strode down the sidewalk, gaze on the house at the end.

"Shepherd," Ryan answered.

"Hey, honey," Heather said. "We've got a situation here on Heritage Street. I just heard several screams coming from Number 306. I'm checking it out, but I think you should send a car down here."

"On it," Ryan replied.

Heather hadn't technically seen anything to indicate danger – it could be a woman freaking out about a mouse or something – but it was better to be safe than sorry, always.

She opened the low gate which led up to the house and stepped onto the path.

The front door burst open, and a woman rushed out, pale as a sheet of flattened fondant. She ripped at her pale pink apron and tore it off. "Oh my, gosh," she yelped.

Heather stepped into her path and held out her palms. "Whoa, there," she said. "What's going on? Are you all right."

The woman tugged at a lock of graying hair and shook her head. "Oh my gosh, Mr. Jones. Not Mr. Jones."

"Slow down," Heather said and patted the air. "It's all right. You're safe." She glanced over the maid's shoulder and up at the front door, which had swung shut behind her. "Is there a danger?"

The woman nodded.

"Is there someone trying to hurt you? Mr. Jones?"

The woman shook her head. "It's a snake."

Relief flooded Heather. Just a silly old snake. But who would name their snake, Mr. Jones? Weird choice for a scaly serpent.

"A snake killed Mr. Jones," the woman said, and wrung her hands.

Heather's relief evaporated into thin air. "Mr. Jones is your employer? Did the snake get out of its cage?"

"No. I mean, yeah, he's my boss, but he didn't own a snake. I don't know where it came from. I've never seen one like that before." She shivered and rubbed her upper arms. "It's all red and yellow all over."

Heather exhaled sharply. That sounded like a Coral Snake. She hadn't seen one of those since she was a kid.

She'd been somewhat fascinated by snakes in middle school.

"Can you do me a favor?" Heather asked.

"Yeah," the woman replied, and trembled from head to toe.

"Stay right here with me. The cops are on their way. They'll get rid of the snake and check if Mr. Jones is all right."

"He's definitely dead," the woman said. Tears welled up in her eyes. "Oh gosh. I only came back because I forgot my purse on the counter, like an idiot, and then he was there. Oh, gosh, I think I'm going to be sick."

"Just breathe," Heather said and stroked the maid's back. "Breathe. Everything is going to be all right."

Not necessarily true. They'd have to catch the poisonous snake and figure out how it'd gotten in there in the first place.

The cruiser whooped behind her and flashed its lights. The maid transformed into a gibbering mess and sobbed, uncontrollably.

Perhaps it was relief at the arrival of an authority figure.

Ryan got out of the car. "What's going on?"

Heather licked her lips. "I think you should call Snake Control."

Chapter 3

The guy in the tan uniform slammed the back doors of his van closed, then turned and tipped his hat toward Heather and Ryan.

The stark, black lettering, Hillside Snake Rescue, stood out on the side of the vehicle.

"That's that," Ryan said. "Snake is out of the way, and Mr. Jones has been taken for his autopsy."

Heather grimaced. "The minute I heard it was a Coral Snake, I knew it was done. Such a pity."

Ryan nodded, then unhooked his thumbs from his pockets and

gestured up toward the house. "Shall we?"

"Yeah, I've got time. I just checked in with Amy, and they're both fine. Lilly's making popcorn again. She's insisted on a movie afternoon."

Ryan chuckled, then led the way up the path to the front porch. He stomped up the stairs and to the door, then creaked it open and disappeared inside.

Heather followed him, but her frown didn't disappear. Sheesh, at this rate she'd end up with wrinkles on top of wrinkles. She'd be one giant wrinkle by the age of seventy.

"Coral snake," Ryan said. "I'll have to research those. I don't know much about our slithering brethren in Texas."

"That's what bothered me," Heather replied. "Not your lack of serpentine knowledge, I mean, but the fact that there was a coral snake indoors. These are the kind of snakes that spend most of their time underground."

"Oh yeah?"

"Yeah. I could understand if the snake had burrowed under the guys front porch, and he was down there and got bitten by accident, but here? In his living room?" Heather shook her head and glanced around at the beige living room furniture and the potted plant in the corner. "It just doesn't make sense to me."

Ryan walked around to the spot where the victim had fallen. "So, you're saying this might have been a... manufactured scenario?"

"Maybe. I don't know. All I'm saying is it doesn't make sense," Heather replied. "Let's take a look around."

"Good idea," Ryan replied. He walked toward the fireplace at the end of the room and peered past the grate. "You don't think it could've slipped through here?"

"Through a chimney? No." Heather strode toward the back door in the kitchen, then tried it. Locked up tight. The key hung on a hook on the wall, out of reach from the window.

She glanced at the window pane, then froze. What was that?

"Hon, come take a look at this," she said, and her footsteps clicked across the plain, white tiles.

"What is it?" Ryan asked and jogged up to her. "A snake hole?"

"Maybe." Heather pointed at the window and the netting which had been installed on the outside of it. "Someone's opened a hole in the netting. And it's definitely big enough for a coral snake."

"Window's open, too," Ryan said. "Looks like this might be our entry point."

Heather paced back and forth in front of the kitchen counter. The more she considered the scenario, the less sense it made that a snake would randomly slip into this man's house and attack him.

Snakes didn't behave that way unless provoked. Even a notoriously aggressive rattlesnake wouldn't go out of its way to track down a potential victim.

Heather hurried to the keys beside the door, grabbed them, then unlocked and opened up.

She stepped into the back garden and Ryan followed, hot on her heels.

They stopped beside the window, and Heather bent and stared at the flower bed. "Footprints. Shoe prints. Small and flat."

"I'm going to have to get some of the boys down here to help me process this scene. Looks like we've just upgraded the case from accident to homicide," Ryan said, then sighed. "Man, these things get more complicated each week."

"A snake. Why not just poison the guy with a cookie or something?" Heather rammed her mouth shut. She'd reached the point of no return. The thought of murder in her hometown didn't scare her anymore. It injected her with determination.

"Revenge killing," Ryan said, immediately. "That's the first thing that comes to mind."

"What? Why?"

"Mr. Jones, sorry, Jimmy Bob Jones, was a poacher," Ryan said. "We've been to his house several times to investigate, but he manages to hide his operation every time."

"Jimmy Bob Jones," Heather said, and palmed her face.

"JB for short. We've had a lot of complaints about this guy," Ryan replied. He shook his head. "Given what we know now, it's time we look more closely at those complaints."

Heather whipped out her notepad and pen, then scribbled the victim's name across the top of the page. She tapped her bottom lip with the end of the pen. "A revenge killing. That begs the question, who would have access to a coral snake? Who would know how to handle a coral snake without getting bitten?"

"I can think of one place in town," Ryan replied. "The Sunny Hill Pet Store. They stock exotic critters too, as far as I know. I can't remember the owner's name, but she was definitely one of the folks who complained about the poacher."

Heather scribbled the pet store's name down on her notepad. "I'll be sure to check that out."

"Right," Ryan said. "I'm gonna head to the car and call this in."

"Yeah, I'd better get home and stop Lilly from devouring her own body weight in popcorn. You know how she gets," Heather replied.

The girl had a fantastic metabolism, but she took advantage of it far too often and in the worst ways.

Dave and Lilly loved their junk food.

"I'd like to see you stop her." Ryan laughed and looped his arm around his wife's shoulders.

"Oh, I'll figure out a way. I'll threaten her with a broccoli bake for dinner."

Ryan burst out laughing again. "Pure evil."

Chapter 4

Heather unlocked the front door of Donut Delights and flipped the sign from closed to open.

Amy stood behind the counter and fiddled with the coffee machine. "Ugh, I need a double espresso this morning."

"Espresso?" Heather asked, and turned to face her bestie.

"Fine, a double cappuccino. You know I can't stand that bitter, stuff," Amy replied, and stifled another yawn. She punched a few buttons, then clicked mugs onto the metal grate beneath the spouts of the machine.

Heather strode to the counter, then rounded it and plonked down in her stool. "Almost time for the morning rush. I wonder who our first customer will be today."

The beginning of the day always intrigued Heather. Fingers of yellow-orange dawn crept across the tarmac outside and touched the windows of the store opposite the road.

"I think I'm allergic to waking up this early," Amy said and turned on the milk frothing machine.

The front door to Donut Delights opened, and the bell tinkled overhead.

Heather straightened and hopped off her seat, though she had barely any energy. She'd spent the night pondering yesterday's 'snake murder.'

A familiar face had entered the store.

"Jamie?" Heather asked. She'd interviewed this guy a couple of weeks ago during the case of the murdered Private Investigator.

Jamie Purdue stepped up to the counter and smiled at her. He glanced at Amy, and she met his gaze and fumbled with the frothing machine. She switched it off, coughed into her fist, then smiled. "Hello," she said.

Very un-Amy-like. She'd usually have a witty quip at this point in the conversation.

"Hi," he said and returned her smile.

Heather glanced between the two of them. What was this awkward vibe about?

Amy noticed her gaze and returned to their cappuccinos. She poured the foam on top and used the spoon to spread it, evenly.

"May I help you, Mr. Purdue?" Heather asked.

"You can call me Jamie," he replied. "I – uh, I'm not here for donuts."

"Coffee?" Heather asked.

Amy jumped at the mention of coffee. Something had gotten under her skin. What on earth was it?

"No, thank you," Jamie said and glanced at Heather's bestie again. "I've come to talk about JB Jones."

Heather arched an eyebrow. "Oh really?"

"Yeah, I figured you'd be investigating this case. I read about it in the paper this morning. I've got some information for you." Jamie pressed his fingertips onto the glass counter.

"I'm all ears," Heather replied.

Amy placed the cappuccino on the counter in front of her. Heather swept it up into her hands and took a huge sip. The warm coffee slid down her throat, and she sighed.

That was much better.

"Let's sit down," Heather said and circled the counter. She walked toward one of her wrought iron tables, then drew back a chair and sat down. She placed her cup on the glass top.

Jamie joined her a second later. Ames stayed behind the counter, her cheeks tinged pink.

Heather would have to quiz her about this later.

"What's up?" Heather asked.

Jamie placed his hands on the table and brushed them over each other. "I started working at the Sunny Hill Pet Store about a week ago," he said. "I like it there. I love animals, and this fit the bill for a great job."

"Right?" Was this a segue to something else? "And you heard about Jones' murder."

"I assumed I'd be a suspect. We have a collection of exotic and local snakes in store. There are a few collectors who come from far and wide to purchase them. In fact, my boss, Sofia, wants to set up a fund for coral snakes."

"A fund?"

"Yeah. She wants to invest research into expanding the genetic diversity among local snake populations," Jamie said.

"You lost me for a second there," Heather replied, then chuckled. "So basically, she wants to protect these snakes?"

"Yeah, something like that. Though, I'm kinda off the point here," Jamie said.

Heather shifted and took another sip of her drink.

"Did you know that there hasn't been a death reported from a coral snake bite since 1967? That's when the antivenin was developed, I believe." Jamie scratched his stubbly chin and folded his arms across his broad chest. "One of those snakes went missing from our store two days before Jones died."

"That's quite a lot to process," Heather said. She patted down her apron and brought out her notepad and pen. She always carried it with her, for times like these.

Leads could pop up at a moment's notice.

"And there's more," Jamie said. He checked that there weren't any customers incoming, then leaned in. "I witnessed an argument between my boss,

Sofia, and Jones the morning of his death."

"What was said?" Heather asked.

"Sofia accused him of poaching snakes near the South Bosque River. Cottonmouth snakes, to be specific, and he laughed in her face." Jamie grimaced. "It was right outside the store."

"Did he come around often?" Heather asked. If Jones had been determined to annoy Sofia, it stood to reason that she might've snapped.

But would a woman who loved snakes risk endangering one to end the poacher's life? After all, there hadn't been any real guarantee that the snake would bite the poacher. That'd been serendipity for the animals of Hillside and an unfortunate turn of events for Jimmy Bob Jones.

"I don't think so. I didn't see him prior to yesterday morning, but boy, when he walked past Sofia lost it. She was furious at him and just launched an attack. Verbal, of course." Jamie ran his hand through his thick brown hair. "It sounds like I'm trying to incriminate my boss, but that's not it. I just want to be helpful. The last time you investigated, I wasn't exactly cooperative, and the killer almost got away."

"I appreciate it, Jamie," Heather said and flashed him a smile. She wrote down a few notes, then underlined Sofia's name. "I think you'll be seeing a lot more of me, soon. And Amy, too."

Jamie's cheeks reddened. "Good. I – uh, I look forward to talking with you both again."

Chapter 5

Ryan squashed in beside Heather on the bleachers and handed her a stick with a blob of bright pink cotton candy on the end.

"You know," he said and gestured with his own blue colored blob. "I didn't think they'd have treats at a dog show. Not the human kind, anyway."

Eva Schneider shifted beside Heather and opened the Donut Delights box she'd brought along for her snack. "Who needs cotton candy when you can have one of Heather's fantastic Iced Pumpkin Donuts?"

"I'll have one," Amy said and twiddled her fingers toward the box.

Eva slapped her fingers away. "Ah! What's the magic word, dear?"

"Puh-lease." Amy grinned and removed a treat from the box, then took a bite. "Oh yeah. That's Thanksgiving on the tongue."

Heather craned her neck above the crowds of people and searched for Lilly. The contestants had lined up on the opposite side of the field, nearby a small decorative gate which led to a complicated course.

Dave sat beside Lilly and wagged his tail, totally calm.

"Dave is a changed dog thanks to that girl," Eva said.

"He still pees on my carpets," Amy replied. "He hasn't changed that much."

All four of them laughed together.

"Hey hon," Ryan said. "We got the results back from those shoes. A woman's size seven. Too small to be a man's."

"So, the killer was a woman," Heather said and bit her bottom lip. At least, this distracted her from her nerves for Lilly and Dave's performance. "A woman who despised the poacher."

"Or a man trying to frame a woman."

Heather's mind flicked back to Jamie Purdue in Donut Delights. He'd seemed sincere, but why had he sought her out? Could it be that he'd come to see her to throw her off his tracks?

She'd dealt with killers who'd have done exactly that to get away with, well, murder.

An elderly woman shuffled onto the field, just ahead of the bleachers and raised a megaphone. "Quiet, now. The contest is about to begin." Impatience tinged the woman's sweet tone.

"Oh yeah, this is going to be awesome. Lils and Dave will be the stars of the show," Amy said.

Heather crossed her fingers in her lap. "Why am I so nervous?" She muttered to her husband.

Ryan kissed her on the cheek. "Because she's your daughter. You want what's best for her."

The old woman walked to the center of the small field and raised the megaphone again. "Ladies and gentlemen, welcome to the annual Fall Fur Flurry!"

Applause ruptured the torpid silence.

The woman waved her hands for quiet, and it fell once again. "Our contestants will compete on this course. The dog and owner to finish first and with the least number of technical mistakes will win our grand prize."

"Ooh, what's the grand prize?" Amy hissed and took another bite of her donut.

The scent of cinnamon and dog shampoo twisted through the air and up Heather's nostrils. It was a strange combination, but she liked it.

"The first place winner will walk away with a fully paid dog training course and," the woman said, and paused for effect, "a fully paid family trip to New York to attend the Leatherstocking Cluster Fall Dog Show!"

"Wow," Heather said and clasped Ryan's hand. "Wow, wouldn't that be exciting?"

"Like you could ever leave Donut Delights," Ryan whispered back.

He had a good point, but if Lilly and Dave one, she'd be hard-pressed to say no to their newest family member.

"Our second place prize is a cash prize of two hundred dollars, written out to the owner, to be used at local grooming salons and pet stores. Third place is a voucher for a dog spa worth fifty dollars."

Heather gobbled down some cotton candy, but it did nothing to soothe her nerves.

Lilly the star probably hadn't registered any nerves at this point.

The girl had left the house in her Halloween costume, Indiana Jones, with Dave dressed as her research assistant.

"Contestants will be judged according to a point and timing system. There are three judges," the woman said. "I am Penelope Walsh. Our second judge is Jerry Lee Lobos, and our third is Kiara Tinny." She gestured to the folks at the table beside the obstacle course.

"Oh my gosh, this lady likes the sound of her own voice," Amy groaned. "I wish they'd start already. I can't take the waiting. Really gets my nerves up."

"And without further ado, I'll introduce our first contestant. Miss Lilly Jones and her doggy pal, Dave."

Penny Walsh hurried over to the judging table and took her seat.

"She's first," Heather said, then grasped Ryan's hand and squeezed. "It's better that way, right? She can just get it out of the way and relax."

Lilly stepped up to the cute, carved gate and clicked her

fingers at Dave. He rose from his sitting position and wagged his tail, once.

Lilly bent and removed his leash.

She opened the gate, then directed Dave toward the first obstacle – a long tunnel.

Dave jostled through it and popped out the other end. Lilly ran alongside him and fed him a treat, then patted the end of a long balance beam.

He hopped up and pattered along its length, no barks sounded. Not a single complaint.

"Are we one hundred percent sure that's Dave out there?" Ryan asked.

"I've never seen anything like it," Heather replied. "He's fantastic."

Lilly clicked again, and Dave hopped off the balance beam. He turned a circle, barked and leaped into the air.

The crowd applauded.

Lilly directed him through several traffic cones, left, right, left until Heather's head spun from the changes in direction.

The course continued, and Dave went through each obstacle. He stumbled and fell once, but hopped up and resumed the course. A true champion.

Lilly stopped in front of the judge's table and bowed. Dave

rose on his hind legs and barked once, then dropped back down.

The crowd cheered and whooped. The judges scribbled down their scores.

Chapter 6

Heather stopped Lilly in front of the pet store and place a hand on her daughter's shoulder. "You know I'm super proud of you, right?"

"We all are," Amy said and grinned from beside the door. "Our very own heroin."

"I only got second place," Lilly replied. "But I'm super excited to get Dave some cool stuff." She took out her prize money and flashed it at the pair of them. "Maybe a new doggy cushion? Or a ball? Or, oh, one of those milk bone things."

"Let's go inside and check it out," Heather said. She opened the front door of the Sunny Hill Pet Store.

They stepped out of the Hillside afternoon and into the scent of wood shavings, feathers, dog food and all those other pet store smells that sent Heather right back to the day she'd brought Dave home as a puppy.

Lilly grinned and disappeared among the toys and cages. She was on a mission of her own.

"Look at her go," Amy said and folded her arms across her chest. "She really is a mini-you, Heather. A total go-getter."

"Stop, you're making me blush."
Heather patted her bestie on the
back, then turned to the counter.

A woman stood behind it, beside
a dogfood display. A collection of
fluffy toys for cats sat on top of
the wood, in front of her.

"May I help you?" She asked.

It wasn't a coincidence Heather
had chosen the Sunny Hill Pet
Store for Lilly's shopping
adventure.

"Are you Sofia?" Heather asked,
and extended her hand.

A frown flickered across the
woman's forehead. She swept
her dark hair back, then shook
Heather's hand. "Sofia Lopez,

yes. I'm the owner of this store. How may I help you?"

"Is Jamie here?" Amy asked, then rammed her teeth together to block any further questions.

Sofia blinked at her. "No, his shift ended an hour ago. Do you want me to take a message for you?"

Amy shook her head but didn't say anything.

Heather narrowed her eyes at her best friend. She'd have to have a chat with Amy sooner rather than later. Her behavior had upgraded from mildly strange to downright weird.

"Miss Lopez," Heather said. "Do you have a minute to chat?"

Amy sauntered backward and bumped into a parrot cage. The bird squawked at her, and she yelped. "I'm going to go check on Lilly."

"Sure," Sofia said and focused on Heather rather than the commotion her bestie had made. "Do you need help with your pet? I can't offer medical advice, unfortunately."

"No, nothing like that," Heather replied. She brought out her notepad and pen, then scratched Sofia's name across the top of the page.

"You a reporter?"

"I'm a private investigator working in conjunction with the Hillside Police Department."

"I see," Sofia replied. "And you want to ask me about the break-in?"

"I – pardon me?"

Sofia gestured to the back of the store. "We had a break-in a few days ago. Someone stole a very valuable snake. I believe Jamie reported it to the police."

Heather made a note of that. Ryan sure hadn't mentioned anything about a break-in being reported, and he would have, given that they'd discussed the pet store directly after the discovery of JB's body.

"I came to discuss the murder of the poacher, Jimmy Bob Jones."

"Oh," Sofia said. "Yeah, I read about that in the paper. To be honest, I'm not unhappy about it. He was a horrible creature."

"Why do you say that?" Heather asked, pen poised above paper.

Sofia sighed and reached up to massage her shoulder with one hand. "Because he was a poacher. He hunted animals for their fur or skin. He decimated the local populations around here." Sofia ground her teeth until they squeaked. "I despised him."

"Is that what you fought about on the morning of his murder?" Heather asked.

"That's correct," she replied, without shame. "He was outside my pet store, and I chased him off."

"Why?" Heather asked.

"I believe he was the one who stole my coral snake," Sofia replied.

Her coral snake. The snake had definitely come from the store then. It was too much coincidence bundled into one scenario. "Ma'am, are you aware how Mr. Jones was murdered?"

"No," Sofia said. "Jamie mentioned something happened to him, but I'm not one for reading the papers. Too much bad news. I get anxiety from them."

She could totally relate to that. "He was bitten by a coral snake."

"I knew he stole it," Sofia hissed and made a fist.

"The snake was removed by the Hillside Snake Removal services, so you might want to give them a call," Heather said.

Sofia moved to grab the receiver of her phone, but Heather held up her pen, and she stopped.

"But it's become quite clear that this wasn't an accidental death. It was a murder. The snake was slipped into Jones' home by someone else."

Sofia's brow wrinkled again. Her liquid brown eyes danced in their sockets. "Who?"

"That's exactly what I intend on finding out." Heather flipped her notepad and shut and slipped it into her back pocket. "Miss Lopez, do you have an alibi for the time of the murder."

"What time was it?"

"Late afternoon, around about this time," Heather replied.

"Oh, that's easy. I was right here in the store. I always am until closing time," Lopez replied. "I had a few customers too. You're welcome to call them to confirm that they saw me."

"That would be very helpful," Heather replied.

Sofia scribbled down a few numbers on a piece of paper. "They'll have receipts for their purchases too, so you know I'm not lying." She handed the information over to Heather.

"Thank you," Heather replied, and accepted the paper. Strange, she was used to a struggled when it came to interviewing suspects.

So far, everything had fallen into her lap.

"I'm going to call my husband," Heather said. "He works at the station and he'll check whether your break-in was reported or not. If not, we'll check it out and make sure that snake gets back to you."

"Thank you," Sofia said. "It belongs here. Well, it belongs in the wild, and I'll feel a lot more comfortable letting it go free, now that I know that poacher is gone."

The woman had definitely had the motivation to murder Jones.

"Don't get me wrong." Sofia tucked her hair behind her ear. "I despised him, but I'm not the type of person who could ever hurt –"

Lilly darted up to the front of the store and help up a little squirming bundle of fur. "Please, Au-Heather. Please, please. Dave needs a companion."

"What is that?" Heather asked.

"It's a kitten," Lilly replied, and indignation crept into her tone. How dare Heather not recognize a cat?

"Oh no. No, no, no." She'd never been a cat person.

"Please!" Lilly whined. "Dave would love a friend."

"A dog friend," Heather said. "Not a kitty."

"I'll look after her, and feed her and I'll make sure they don't fight. Oh, please!" Lilly clasped the kitten to her chest and kissed its furry head.

Heather could kind of see the appeal. It had big blue eyes and soft white fur.

"Fine," Heather said, at last. "But you're going to have to explain this to Ryan."

"I will," Lilly said and dashed past her toward the counter.

Amy stepped up beside Heather, her arms folded. "You realize what that cat looks like, don't you?"

"Huh? No?"

Amy's lips twitched, and she pressed them together. "My white fur carpets." And she burst out laughing.

Chapter 7

Heather rearranged her coat and clutched it to her chest. She stamped her feet in her boots and stared up at the sign of the pet store. The early morning wind whipped against her cheeks.

Ryan knocked on the front door of the store, and Sofia appeared behind the smiling cat sign. She waved once, then unlocked and let them in.

"Thanks for coming," she said. "I appreciate it. The sooner I can get my snake back, the better."

"That's a strange opener," Ryan said. "You're welcome, ma'am."

Sofia beckoned for Heather to come in and she did. She blew hot air into her hands, then shook them out. "Can you show us where the snake, uh, lived?" Heather asked. "The snake's tank, I mean."

"Right this way," Sofia said. She swept toward the back of the store, past the shelves of food, supplements, and toys then stopped in the snake section.

Tanks surrounded them. A few bore red lights to warm their hosts, others plain white. The tops of the tanks were firmly secured and padlocked.

"Padlocks," Heather muttered.

"Yeah," Sofia replied, then pointed to an empty tank. "This is where we kept the coral. The padlock is totally gone. Either they broke it and took it with them, or someone had the key. Except the key isn't missing." Sofia wriggled her lips from side-to-side.

"Who else had access to the key?" Ryan asked, and walked to the cage. He bent and examined the empty insides, then whipped out his flashlight. He clicked it on and shone it on the glass at an angle.

"Jamie, my assistant. But he wouldn't steal a snake. He's terrified of going near that cage at the best of times," Sofia replied.

She scratched the back of her neck, then folded her arms and leaned against a shelf.

"Heather, take a look at this," Ryan said and crooked his finger.

She hurried forward and examined the glass under his flashlight. "Smudges everywhere," she muttered.

"We try to clean the cages as often as possible, but we kinda neglected that one after the break-in. Didn't want to tamper with the evidence." Sofia shrugged. "Honestly, I expected you guy's way sooner."

Except Jamie Purdue hadn't actually reported the break-in, according to Ryan.

"Smudges," Heather muttered and interlaced her fingers. "Interesting."

"You know what it means?"

"Smudges mean fingerprints," Heather said. "And fingerprints are solid evidence."

Ryan nodded once then clicked off his flashlight and rose from the crouch. "We'll have to get a team down here to dust the tank."

"Sofia," Heather said, and licked her lips. "Do you have any idea how the thief got into the store?"

"Oh yeah! They broke in through the back window," Sofia said and pointed toward a door which provided them a glimpse of an office beyond. "I don't have a lock on the office door because we don't keep anything in there but a couple chairs and paperwork."

Heather chewed her bottom lip. "I see. I think I'd better take a walk around the back."

"Sure," Sofia said. "Be my guest."

Ryan followed Heather back out the front of the store, then down into the side alley. They rounded the back of the building and stopped beside a broken window.

"She's awfully helpful," Ryan said, in a monotone.

"Hush," Heather whispered, and pointed toward the open window. The woman could be on the other side, and she was definitely still a suspect, helpful or not.

Heather bent and examined the dirt beneath the window. A shoeprint remained, dried in a bit of mud beneath it, though it was the front portion only.

"Looks the same to me," Ryan said. "But we can't be sure until we get the results back. I'll call this in. It's obviously related to the murder. We don't want to take chances with anything here."

Heather nodded but didn't tear her eyes from the shoeprint. This killer had been careless. They'd left a trail behind and –

Metal glinted along the base of the wall, near a dumpster. Heather pushed herself up and walked to it. She shook her head. Very careless.

"I found the padlock," she said. "Looks like it's been cut with a bolt cutter or something."

"Good detective work as usual," Ryan called back. "I have to call this in."

She gave her husband a thumbs up, then turned her attention back to the padlock. "Why were you so careless?" She muttered, under her breath. "Is it because you didn't care? Because you wanted to get caught?"

This was the hallmark of a killer who wanted attention, or one who had no idea how to commit a murder and cover their tracks.

A desperate plea for help or a downright lack of care.

Heather chewed the corner of her lip. Ugh, she had to get back to Donut Delights anyway. She'd think about it on the walk over there.

Chapter 8

Heather strolled down the road and turned her face toward the sun and let it warm her cheeks.

The case confused her. It should've been straight up and down, simple to a fault. They had to find the person who'd stolen the snake and slipped it through the hole in the netting of Jones' back window.

Except, any person who stole a snake had to be very brave, very stupid or have a lot of experience with snakes.

Which meant the two main suspects were Jamie, who hadn't reported the break-in, but had told her about it straight up, and Sofia, who had a rock solid alibi.

Ryan had called each of the people who'd seen her at the time of the murder, and they'd all had receipts for their purchases and confirmed her presence in the store.

Heather pursed her lips and tucked her hands into her pockets.

She stifled a yawn and her eyes teared up.

Dave had kept her up all night, whining because the new kitten, Cupcake, had taken up a spot on Lilly's pillow.

Heather rubbed her eyes and bumped into a pole.

"Ouch," she said and stepped back a pace. She rubbed the bump on her forehead.

A lamppost glared right back at her. Someone had pasted a flier to its metal side, and Heather had managed to crumple the bottom of it on impact.

BEWARE THE POACHER!

Heather raised her eyebrows at the bold font title. Interesting.

She whipped it off the lamppost then straightened it out.

"There is a poacher in our town. Keep your animals indoors. He will steal your cats and dogs for their fur. Call Penny Walsh to report sightings of the Poacher," Heather read, out loud.

The bottom of flier flaunted removable tabs, each with Penelope Walsh's name and number printed in bold font.

"Penelope Walsh," Heather whispered. "Why is that name so familiar?" She cast her mind back, then froze.

Of course! Penelope Walsh had been one of the judges at Lilly and Dave's dog show. The elderly woman with the megaphone.

"Hmm, I didn't get a close enough look." Heather rubbed her forehead again, then dug in her pocket and brought out her cell.

She held up the flier and typed the number into her phone, then pressed the green icon.

She placed the phone against her ears.

Two rings, and then. "Hello?" Penelope's voice brought back memories of cotton candy and nerves.

"Hi, is this Penelope Walsh?"

"That's correct," she replied. "May I help you with something?"

"Penelope, my name is Heather Shepherd. I've just picked up one of your fliers in town and –"

"Oh, about the poacher?" Penny asked. "I'm afraid I forgot to take those down. Unfortunately, the poacher has passed on from this world. There's no need to report his movements anymore. Your dog or cat is safe."

"I have both now," Heather said, though she hadn't meant to. "And actually, I'm calling regarding the poacher's death."

"Oh?" Penny hummed on the other end of the line. "I'm afraid I won't be able to help much with that."

"Mrs. Walsh, I'm working with the Hillside Police Department to solve the murder case," Heather said.

"Please, call me Penelope," she replied. "I'll help in whatever way I can, though I don't know I'll be of any service."

"Did you know Mr. Jones, personally?" Heather asked, and continued her walk toward Donut Delights. She turned her head so the wind wouldn't whistle in the phone.

"Not personally, no. I may have met him once, but the conversation certainly didn't last long. I don't collude with people of his ilk if you catch my drift."

"You're an animal enthusiast," Heather replied. She pinned the cell phone between her ear and shoulder, then folded up the flier and tucked it into her pocket.

"That's correct. I prefer my animals living and happy, thank you very much," Mrs. Walsh said.

"I share that opinion with you, Penelope," Heather said, and smiled, but her sleuth sense forced her to push a little more, a little further. "What made you decide to put up these fliers?"

"I spotted that horrific man on one of my walks along the South Bosque. They keep me fit, you know. I often take Pebbles with me, for fun. He's my Labrador."

"I see," Heather said, then grasped her phone in her hand again. She checked up and down the street, then darted across and toward the road which led to her store. "What happened then?"

"I saw him fiddling with something at the edge of the river. Pebbles went crazy, barking and whining at the end of the leash. Anyway, that horrible poacher heard and turned around. He had a – oh gosh. He had a bloodied knife in one hand. He'd obviously just murdered an innocent animal," Penelope said and choked back tears. Or nausea.

It might've been both.

"I'm so sorry you had to see that," Heather said. She truly was. That would've made her both furious and nauseous.

"I am too. Anyway, I yelled at the man then led my Pebbles out of there before he could hurt the dog too. That man was a danger to society. He was a danger to us all," Penelope said.

Heather halted in front of Donut Delights and waved at Amy behind the counter. "What happened after that?"

"Well, that was last week. After that, nothing. I didn't see him or hear much, apart from some rumors about an argument with Sofia at the pet store. She's a lovely woman," Penny said, in a tone which could only be described as rambling. "Did you know she wants to start a fund for coral snakes? What a dear."

"I had heard that." Penelope Walsh sure was well-informed. "Penelope, thank you so much for your time. I've got to run, now."

"Of course. If you need anything else, call me right away."

Heather hung up, and puzzlement crept through her mind. Everyone was so helpful this week.

It was a nice change from the usual blustering angle her suspects implemented. The trouble was, it made them all look innocent as babies.

Chapter 9

Heather settled on the sofa and couldn't keep the smile off her lips.

Somehow, Lilly had done it. Her kitten, Cupcake, lay draped across the top of her pillow, and Dave had curled up in a ball at her side. All three of them snored and wheezed, in a deep sleep.

"Lilly sure has got the magic touch," Amy said and shifted on the couch beside Heather. "Two days and the dog and cat are already comfortable with each other."

"I wouldn't say comfortable," Heather replied. "Every time Lilly says Cupcake, Dave's ears twitch. Look!"

Dave's ears flick-flacked at the mention of it.

"Maybe that's because he likes cupcakes," Amy replied.

"True. That's kind of why I forbade Lilly from calling the cat donut."

Dave's ears twitched again, then settled.

"You know how the dog is with sweets and junk food." Heather couldn't keep the humor from her tone. Dave's antics cheered her up, no matter the situation.

She stretched her legs, then grabbed the remote and pointed it at the TV. She turned down the volume, then faced her bestie on the sofa.

"Uh oh," Amy said. "Am I in trouble? You look super serious."

"I've meant to talk to you."

"About the case?" Amy asked, and picked a popcorn kernel from the bottom of the plastic bowl in her lap.

"Yeah, but not right now."

"Oh," Amy said, then heaved a sigh. "What's up?"

"Amy, I kinda noticed you acting strangely at the beginning of this week. Around one person" Heather said.

"Jamie," Amy replied, immediately. "I know. I acted like a teenage girl. I have a crush on him."

"But what about Kent?" Heather asked.

"Kent broke up with me on Sunday." Amy forced a smile, then waved her hand at Heather. "Don't look at me like that. I'm fine. I'm really fine. I can't say I didn't see it coming. We drifted apart."

"Are you sure you're okay?" Heather asked, and scooched

closer to her bestie. She grasped Amy's hand and squeezed.

"I swear, I'm fine. We'd really become friends more than partners. It wasn't like you and Ryan at all." Amy bit her bottom lip and glanced at the screen. The credits rolled on yet another dinosaur movie. She set down the popcorn bowl on the coffee table. "I want to find what you have, one day. But I guess that's not going to happen anytime soon, and I'm okay with that."

"Oh, Ames," Heather said and grabbed her bestie. She pulled her into a tight hug.

"Don't 'oh, Ames' me yet. It's not like I'm eighty or something."

Amy chuckled and patted Heather's back, then pulled out of the embrace. "Besides, I've got so much to keep me busy. The bakery, Lilly's visits and being your assistant during investigations. Phew." She wiped imaginary sweat from her brow. "It's been a wild ride so far."

Heather chuckled and sat back on the sofa. She grabbed a warm blanket and tucked it around her shoulders.

"What about the case?" Amy asked. "How's that going."

"I want to say easy, but no, it's confusing."

"Why?" Amy reached for her soda and slurped some through the straw. "I thought you said everyone's being really helpful."

"That's the thing," Heather replied. "Everyone is super helpful, but that's confused me anymore. They're all suspects, but they're not behaving like angry killers. Their reactions have been moderate and identical."

"And that's a problem," Amy said.

"Yeah, because this was clearly a revenge killing of some sort, and usually that means an angry person on a war path." Heather rolled her neck, and her bones cracked.

She grimaced at the noise and straightened.

"They can't all be easy."

"No they can't," Heather said. "Here's what gets to me. The killer stole the snake from the pet store, which means the killer had to have known the snake was there."

"Sure. I can see how that doesn't exactly rule out anyone."

"Right, all our suspects are animal lovers." Heather shifted again. Man, she couldn't get comfortable tonight. "But the thief had to have known how to handle a snake or had to have had the right equipment for it."

"Both."

"So –"

"Wait a second," Amy said and raised her index finger. "How do we know the killer and the thief are the same person? The thief could've been hired by the killer, for instance."

"That's a great theory, but it doesn't pan out. You see, the killer wore a certain set of shoes, and Ryan confirmed that the shoe prints outside the pet store were identical," Heather said. "So, unless the thief got a foot transplant…"

"I see your point," Amy said and dropped her hand to her lap. "I don't know what to tell you. To me, it seems like you need more evidence."

"Precisely." Heather crumpled the blanket in her lap. "Luckily, they took fingerprints at the scene. Which means we'll get our evidence. I just hope it makes sense."

"You'll find a way to work it out, Heather," Amy said and winked. "You always do."

Chapter 10

Ryan jived along to the rhythm of the music in Dos Chicos. He clicked his fingers then tapped his fingertips on the edge of the table and smiled at Heather. "You okay, gorgeous?"

"I'm fine," she replied. "It's nice to have a date night." But her thoughts scratched through the facts of the case and searched for answers.

She couldn't switch off once one had started. It was both a good and a bad thing. On the one hand, she wouldn't stop until she'd solved it, on the other, she couldn't stop, and it exhausted her.

The waitress arrived at the table and placed two plates in front of them: soft shell tacos and Heather's quesadillas. Extra cheesy and with a couple of jalapenos thrown into the mix.

She grabbed one of the perfect tortilla triangles and dipped into her tiny pot of salsa, then delivered it to her mouth.

"Delicious," she muttered and chewed. The cheesy goodness spread through her mouth, accented by the zap of the peppers.

"This is so good," Ryan replied. "I'll never get sick of this place."

"Agreed." Heather descended into silence and focused on her meal. She pushed thoughts of the case aside, but they sat at the fringes of her mind and waited for the opportunity to rush back in.

"I've got news," Ryan said and put down his taco. "We got that results back from the break-in at the pet store."

Heather put down her quesadilla, then grabbed a napkin. She dabbed at her lips. "What did you find?"

"Fingerprints on the tank, as we suspected. A lot of them," Ryan replied. "From four sources."

"Oh boy, my sleuth senses are tingling like crazy." Heather grabbed her soda and drank deeply from it. The fizz cleared the flavor from her tongue.

"Get this, there were fingerprints on that cage from Jamie Purdue, Sofia Lopez, the poacher Jones himself and a woman named Penelope Walsh."

"Are you serious?" Heather gripped her soda until her knuckles turned white. "That presents so many scenarios. Penny Walsh was the judge at Lilly's dog show event. I phoned her about those fliers, remember?"

"I remember. I didn't even fingerprint her for this. She was in the system for a minor misdemeanor." His lips curled upward at the corners.

"Oh my gosh, what was it?"

"She, uh, how do I put this? She was much younger at the time and she, kind of, well, she lay naked in front of a bulldozer to stop construction of a new mall. The area was heavily forested."

"Wow," Heather said. "That's a little extreme."

"Yeah, that's what I thought. Apparently, she was an animal rights activist in her day," Ryan said. He picked up his taco and took a bite, then chewed his way through it.

"Curious." Heather passed her soda from her right hand to her left, then back again. "But this doesn't tell us much at all. Three suspects and the victim touched that cage. We need to figure out the possible scenarios there."

"Absolutely," Ryan said, around a mouthful of Mexican food. "Any ideas?"

"Only speculation. Sofia and Jamie might've touched the cage to clean it or to feed the snake. The poacher, wow, that puzzles me, because Sofia would never have allowed him in the store."

"Which means either Jamie did, or there's something Sofia isn't telling us," Ryan replied.

"Yeah," Heather said. "And there's our old lady activist. She could've visited the store and been intrigued by the snake. She did express a fondness for them when I spoke to her on the phone."

"I see," Ryan said. He tapped his fingers on the edge of the table and wriggled his nose. "Basically, we need more evidence and information on each of these suspects before we can get closer to the truth."

"I agree," Heather said. "The shoeprints were small, a female size, right?"

"Yeah, that or a small man's size," Ryan replied. "The shoe itself was unisex according to the supplier."

"Ugh, that doesn't help us much." Heather grabbed her quesadilla and took a bite.

Gosh, if only she could figure out why the killer would've wanted to murder the man with a snake of all things.

"Here's a thought," Ryan said. "That woman, Penelope, was an animal right's activist. Would she really have endangered a coral snake to a murder a man she despised?"

"That's the common theme here," Heather replied. "Each of them hated the guy, apart from Jamie who was kinda indifferent when we spoke, and each of them definitely loved animals. Maybe we're missing something."

"The maid checked out if that's what you're thinking. She didn't have the same size shoe and no fingerprints on the cage," Ryan replied.

"Not what I was thinking, but it's good to have that information." Heather sighed and ate more of her quesadilla. "Why can't we just ask them what size shoe they wear?"

"Because they could have the same size shoe and not be the killer? We'd have to find that exact pair of shoes, and it's highly unlikely we'll find it in their possession," Ryan said.

"Why?" Heather asked.

"Because we found the shoes in the trash can behind Jimmy Bob Jones' house."

Heather exhaled through her nose. "You didn't tell me that."

"I didn't? I thought I had," Ryan said and scratched at his temple. A little sauce smudged onto his skin. "Sorry, hon."

Heather pursed her lips and pressed them to one side. "I think it would be great if you could send me documentation on your investigation. I feel like I'm flying blind most of the time."

Ryan nodded. "You're absolutely right. I'll bring home a dossier tomorrow. I should've done that kind of thing from the start, but honestly, you move so fast on these investigations I've never needed to in the past."

Heather blushed at the compliment. She cleared her throat and took a sip of soda to cool down. "Anyone could've bought a pair of those shoes and worn them, whether they were too small or too big."

"That's the gist of it, yeah." Ryan grabbed a napkin and brushed off his mouth.

Heather pushed her empty plate aside and narrowed her eyes at the string of cheese draped across it. "Looks like I've got some people to interview."

Chapter 11

"I feel like a stalker," Amy said and clutched her handbag to her side. "We just got off work for heaven's sake, and we're thrown right into the middle of a stalking spree."

"We weren't thrown," Heather replied. "We leaped." She drew Amy toward the park, under the rays of the afternoon sun.

They'd left Donut Delights, locked up and spotted Jamie Purdue just across the road. The man had strolled along without a care. Stalking had ensued.

"And it's not stalking. We're casing him out. I need to talk to him anyway. There are things in this case that just don't add up."

Amy nodded but pressed her lips into a thin line. Perhaps, she didn't like the idea of her semi-crush as the murderer.

Heather stopped beneath a tree and raised her hand to shade her eyes from the glare. The trees stood still, the afternoon was breathless but without heat, and clouds rolled on the horizon.

"There," she whispered, and pointed to the solitary figure on the park bench.

Jamie Purdue held a small bag of bird seed. He sprinkled the grains onto the grass beneath his feet and birds flocked from the trees. They picked at the food and a slow smile spread on Jamie's lips.

"That's sweet," Amy whispered.

"Or creepy," Heather replied.

"I thought I was the cynical one."

Heather snorted, then took off toward the man and his birds. She stopped just short of the animals and folded her arms. Amy rushed up beside her, then halted and cleared her throat.

Jamie looked up at them. "Oh hey, how's it going?"

"Fine, thank you, Mr. Purdue," Heather replied, and dug around in her tote. She brought out her notepad and pen.

"Oh boy. Why do I feel like I'm in school, right now?" Jamie laughed. "I take it you have more questions for me, Mrs. Shepherd."

"Quite a few more" she replied. She scribbled Jamie's name at the top of the page, then frowned.

She'd gone through several notebooks during her investigations. She needed to transition to an electronic device. This much note-taking couldn't be good for the environment.

"Sure, I'll help in whatever way I can. What do you need to know?"

"Why didn't you report the break-in to the cops?" Heather asked, and her pen hovered above the page.

Jamie scattered more birdseed on the ground and frowned at it. "I honestly forgot. The break-in happened, and Sofia didn't treat it like a huge emergency. I thought she would since the coral was missing, but she kinda brushed it off."

Heather wrote down a shorthand version of his answer. "You forgot."

"Yeah, I remember picking up the phone to dial it in, but then another customer came into the store, and I hung up. Totally forgot to call back later," he said and flashed a sheepish smile at them.

Amy didn't make a quip. She just stared at Jamie and kept her mouth shut.

Heather fumbled through her notes, then brought out a picture she'd tucked between the pages. A mugshot from the dossier Ryan had dropped off at Donut Delights that morning.

"Did this woman ever enter the store?" She asked and held up the image of Penelope Walsh. "She would've looked like this but older. She's around sixty now, I think."

"Oh yeah, Mrs. Walsh? She came in a couple of times. She has a lot of cats. But now that you mention it, she did seem really interested in the coral snake. Although, she stared at the rattlesnake a lot, too."

"I see," Heather said and fumbled the picture back into the pages of her notepad.

"Is there anything else?"

"We found your fingerprints on the tank," Heather said, simply.

Jamie placed the birdseed sack to one side and folded his arms. "That's because I clean the case. Admittedly, I do a rush job on the snake tanks because, well, they kinda freak me out. Okay, I'll admit it, they scare me."

"You and me both," Amy said, at last.

"One last thing." Heather stepped closer to Jamie, and a few of the birds fluttered away from the seeds at his feet. "Did you ever see JB Jones in the store? Did he ever come inside?"

Jamie's lips writhed. He looked past Heather at the street, then behind the bench at the line of trees. "Yeah," he whispered. "I didn't want to tell you before because I thought it might incriminate me. I know it's stupid, and it looks worse now, but yeah, he came in."

"What happened?" Heather asked, and lowered her tone.

"I was fiddling around below the counter when the door to the store opened," Jamie said. "I stood up quick, but there was no one there, so I just assumed that whoever it was had gone through to check out the pets."

"Okay," Heather said and wrote the details down. "And then?"

"It was awfully quiet for a long time. Freaked me out. So, I walked down the aisle, and that was when I saw him."

"The poacher?" Amy asked, and swallowed. At least her cheeks hadn't gone pink this time.

"That's right. The poacher. He was right beside the coral snake case. He had his nose pressed up against the things and his palm against it too."

"Oh gosh, that's creepy." Amy shivered and rubbed her upper arms.

"Yeah, that was what I thought," Jamie replied. "So I immediately asked him to leave. Sofia had given him a lifelong ban from the pet store. Yeah, he didn't like that. He started screaming at me."

"What did you do?" Heather asked.

Jamie bowed his head for a moment. "Ugh, look, I'm not proud of the next part."

"Go ahead. You can tell us."

"I picked him up and carried him out of the store," Jamie said. He raised his head again and met Heather's gaze. "I didn't want to call the cops for something like that, so I just bounced him myself."

"You picked up a grown man," Amy said. "I didn't see the body, but I'm assuming the guy wasn't a tiny dude."

"He wasn't the biggest guy I'd ever seen, but yeah. I'm ex-military. You've got to be able to

129

carry heavy loads and think under pressure. Those instincts just kicked in," Jamie replied. He scratched the back of his neck. "He didn't like that at all. Threatened to sue me and the store and the entire world."

"But he never got the chance," Heather said.

Jamie dug into the bird seed again and threw it down. "Nope."

Chapter 12

Heather rapped her knuckles on Penelope Walsh's front door, then tucked a strand of hair behind her ear.

Amy yawned and rattled the donuts around in the box. "Whoops, sorry. I hardly slept last night. I don't know why, but I keep having nightmares."

"What about?" Heather asked.

"That I arrive at your house for a slumber party, and you guys are just gone." Amy shifted to the side of the door and peered at the window beside it. The pale pink curtains blocked her view.

"The house is empty. Totally empty. It's kinda freaky."

"Kinda," Heather said. "Don't worry, Ames, we're not going anywhere."

"I know," Amy replied. "I'd find out about it before you left and stowaway in the trunk of your car." She laughed, but it transformed into a jaw-creaking yawn mid-chuckle.

Heather knocked again. "Maybe she's not home."

Footsteps sounded on the other side of the door. A lock drew back, and the door creaked inward.

Penelope Walsh blinked at them, sleepily. "May I help you?"

Oh, shoot, they probably should've come a little later. It was just past six in the morning. All those early wake-up calls for donuts had desensitized her to the sleep patterns of normal folk.

"Hi, Penelope, I'm so sorry to bother you this early in the morning. I'm Heather Shepherd. We spoke on the phone about the poacher?"

"Are you asking me or telling me?" Penny asked, then forced a weak smile. "Sorry, I'm not a morning person."

Amy stifled a yawn behind her fist. "I hear ya on that one."

"We brought donuts," Heather said and flicked the top of the Donut Delights box.

"That will go well with my morning coffee," Penelope said, then beckoned. "Come on in." She turned and shuffled back into her home.

Heather followed the elderly woman down the dingy hall and into a vast kitchen. She'd never have guessed it'd be in a house as small as Penny's.

"What a lovely place," Heather said.

"Thank you," Penelope replied, and grabbed the pot from the counter. She shuffled across the room and set about the coffee preparations. "You mentioned the poacher?"

Amy strode into the room and placed the donut box on the melamine-topped table, then flipped its lid open and grinned at the glistening Iced Pumpkin donuts nestled inside.

"That's correct," Heather said. "I told you on the phone. I'm investigating in conjunction with the Hillside Police Department. It's come to my attention that you were in the Sunny Hill Pet Store, recently."

"Oh yes, of course, I was," Penelope said. "I visit there often."

Two cats wandered into the room, a tabby and a tortoise shell. They curled around Penny's ankles and meowed up at her. "All right, you two. In a minute." She let the coffee brew and hurried to the cupboard opposite.

The cats trailed after her, still meowing complaints.

"Cute cats," Amy said, and stuck her pink in her ear. She twiddled it around. "Noisy cats."

"I have six," Penelope replied, and brought the kibble down from the counter. She poured it into six different colored bowls, then refilled a large blue water bowl at the end of the row. "Six little darlings."

"You know cats eat people, right?" Amy asked.

"Ames," Heather said.

"What? I'm just saying. I've read about it in the paper before. I guess you could call it good housekeeping."

Penelope stiffened and placed the bag of kibble on the counter. "You were asking about the pet store, Mrs. Shepherd?"

"Yeah, I heard that you were interested in the coral snake at the back of the store," Heather replied.

"I love all creatures, great and small." Penny smiled and hurried back to the coffee pot.

Amy shifted in her seat, then pointed at a plaque on the wall. "I'm sorry to interrupt, but is that a Safari 550 DGR hunting rifle?"

Heather spun around and stared at the gun. Indeed, it was mounted right behind them, the dark wood polished to perfection.

"Ah, you have an eye for weaponry," Penelope said and clicked her fingers. "Wonderful. It was my husband's. He hunted big game in Africa before he died. I've kept it there as a reminder."

Heather swallowed and looked back at the woman. The image of a hunting husband didn't suit activist Penny. "A reminder of what?"

"How guns can be used for good and evil. For protection and the innocent murder of animals," she said.

Amy reeled in her seat. Apparently, she had a difficult time with this too.

"I'm sorry, Mrs. Walsh," Heather said, "I didn't picture you as the type of person who'd allow that kind of thing. The hunting, I mean."

"Oh dear, I didn't allow Mr. Walsh anything. He did what he wanted. He was a very independent man." She sighed and touched her white hair. "He went his own way. And eventually he passed, and his hunting habits weren't a problem in our marriage anymore."

Amy folded her arms and eyed the rifle askance.

Heather whipped out her notepad and jotted down a few notes, but the ink blobbed on the page.

"Coffee?" Penelope asked, and turned back with a broad smile.

Chapter 13

Heather walked between the shelves in the gun store and examined the boxes of shells, the straps, and implements. Gun oils. Items she'd never envisioned existed. Each visit to this store brought another realization.

This time, it was how lost she was when it came to weapons, in general. She had her Taser, though and that'd have to be enough.

Amy hummed a tune and pranced down the aisle toward the counter at the back.

Neon lights buzzed overhead, and a heavy gate clanged

somewhere in the place. A strange smell drifted on the air. She couldn't place it, but it reminded her of her grandfather for some reason.

"Bally Bob!" Amy yelled in a tone of sheer glee.

The old timer popped up from behind the counter. "Amy, you little shooter. Where you been? Ain't seen you in weeks, girl."

"Oh, I've been around. A little busy, you know how it is."

"You come to shoot? I got the range all warmed up for you. Took out one of my favorites this mornin' for some fun," Bally said and blinked three times in rapid succession.

Amy had a gift for befriending weird and wonderful, men and women from all walks of life. She blamed it on her star sign: Aquarius.

Then again, Heather had to be one of those weird and, hopefully, wonderful people.

"Nah, we've come on official business, today, Bally, ol' pal," Ames said, then turned and crooked a finger in Heather's direction. "Are you coming?"

Heather hurried forward and halted in front of the counter. The paraphernalia behind and beneath it overwhelmed the senses. Pepper spray, cartridges, shells, boxes of bullets, Tasers in all shapes and sizes. A pink one, too.

"How can I help you, ma'am?" Bally asked and tipped an invisible cap in Heather's direction.

"I've come to chat to you about a murder case, Bob," Heather said. She brought out her notepad and pen, her trustee investigating implements, and placed them flat on the counter. "I'm sure you heard about the death of Jimmy Bob Jones."

"I did, I did," Bally said, and nodded. He sniffed once, then ran the back of his across his nose. "Deplorable man. Didn't like that son of a gun one bit."

"Why's that?" Amy asked and leaned her forearms on the counter.

"Well, he bought loadsa guns. Rifles, pistol, even a shotgun or too. Man, I couldn't figure out what he'd need 'em all for," Bally said, and scratched at a mark on top of the counter. "Then one of my other customer's tell me that this guy's a poacher."

"What did you do?"

"Well, next time he came into my store, I told him to get out before I kicked him out," Bally replied, then sniffed again. "I don't care for that kinda man. I can understand huntin' for food or needin' protection, but poaching?"

"You have a problem with that?"

"Oh yeah, big time," Bon replied. "Look, I love guns. I love firing 'em. I even love the recoil and the bruises." He chuckled, but it petered off and his expression. "But not when it's used for nefarious purposes n' stuff like that."

"Killing animals for their skins is pretty darn nefarious," Amy said and pursed her lips.

"That it is. That it is." Bally nodded in Amy's direction but kept his gaze glued to Heather's face. "He was furious, of course. Threw a right tantrum out in the street, the big baby. But he wandered off after a while. Not like he could get back in here." He laughed and gestured to the cage-like construction which barred entrance to the store.

"And you never saw him again?" Heather asked.

"Nope. Heard he got murdered, though. By a snake?"

"Yeah," Amy replied.

"Weird way to go."

Heather didn't comment. She wrote down her notes and her mind twisted around the facts. She bent them and examined them, but there wasn't much there, except more evidence that the poacher hadn't been a nice guy.

He was a poacher, though. That was a given.

"Just one more question, Bob," Heather said. She still couldn't bring herself to call him 'Bally.'

"Sure," he said.

"Did a woman named Penelope Walsh every come in here?" It was the real reason they'd come.

The paradox of a hunting rifle in an activist's home had set off alarm bells in Heather's mind. She had to know more about Mrs. Walsh and whether she'd told the truth about that rifle.

"Sure does. Almost every second day," Ballistic Bon replied. "She's one of my best customers, except she's more interested in the shooting range."

"Oh?" Heather asked and exchanged a glance with her bestie.

Amy raised both eyebrows.

"Yeah, she prefers handguns 'n stuff. Nothin' too big. She's a little lady, you know."

"Did she ever tell you why she's interested in learning to shoot?" Heather asked.

"Nope, and she's not learning neither. The woman knows her guns. She shoots for the pleasure of it I'm sure," Bob said. "Kinda weird to see the look on her face when she does it, though."

"What do you mean?"

"I dunno. Everyone has a look when they fire a weapon," Bally replied. "Amy over here just go this deadpan expression. Nothin' scary."

"And you smile when you shoot," Amy said. "But not a creepy

smile. It's like you're happy to be on the range."

"Darn straight," Bob said.

"And Penelope?" Heather asked.

Ballistic Bob touched his finger to his bottom lip. "She got this expression that's like, angry or somethin'. Her face scrunches up real tight." He tried to emulate it, and Amy burst out laughing.

Bally chuckled and rolled his eyes at her. "She never bought a gun from me, though."

Heather made a final note, then capped her pen. "Thank you for your time, Bob. I'll be in touch if I need anything else."

"You come back soon, now. I got a Ruger with your name on it, Amy, girl. Ergonomic Wrap-Around Grip Model. Nine millimeters. Real fancy."

"Thanks, Bally. I'll see you soon," Ames replied, and clapped him on the shoulder.

Chapter 14

Heather strolled down the sidewalk toward the pet store. Puzzle pieces floated around in her mind. They jammed their edges together, turned and tried another composition, but never fell into place.

"Where are we going?" Amy asked.

"Oh, sorry, Ames, I was lost in thought," Heather replied. "Sheesh, I feel like I've been running around headless for the past few days. I've hardly seen the inside of my own store."

"It's all right. Ange and the others have got everything under control. It's just this week's case has been confusing." Amy readjusted her handbag on her shoulder, then glanced up at the gathering clouds. "Looks like it might rain."

"I hope so. It's been pretty dry this week," Heather said. "I've got one last place to visit today, and then we can head back to the store and do what we do best."

"Drink coffee and devour donuts?" Amy asked.

"That too."

Heather strode around the corner and down the road. Thunder rumbled in the dark clouds overhead, and the first fat drops of rain splatted to the concrete. A couple landed on Heather's head.

Amy tilted her face back and accepted the blessing for what it was.

"Here we are," Heather said and stopped in front of the Sunny Hill Pet Store.

The lights were on, but Sofia wasn't behind the counter.

Heather opened the door and stepped inside. An electronic bell chimed in the store, but silence greeted them.

Both women looked up at the small box above the door.

"Well, that's new."

"I'm coming," Sofia yelled from the back.

Amy stepped toward the bird cages, and a frown wrinkled her brow. "It's quiet in here."

"Too quiet," Heather grunted, in a theatrical homage to The Lucky Texan.

Amy clicked her tongue at her bestie but didn't speak again. Instead, she wandered down one of the aisles, further into the pet stores. "Hey, there are goldfish here too."

"Don't tell Lilly," Heather called back. "She'll want to start her own menagerie."

Sofia Lopez hurried to the front of the store and slipped in behind the counter. She brushed the hair from her forehead with the back of her forearm, then exhaled. "May I help you, Mrs. Shepherd?"

"Are you all right?" Heather asked.

Amy popped her head around the corner and scrutinized the owner of the store. "Yeah, you look kinda…"

"Sweaty?" Lopez suggested. "Sorry, I'm spinning because my assistant didn't come in to work this morning."

"Jamie didn't come in for his shift?" Heather asked, and glanced back at Ames.

Her bestie slowly retracted her head from its position and disappeared back down the aisle.

"Yeah, I've been trying to get hold of him but he doesn't answer his home phone or his cell," Sofia replied and shook out her hair. "I don't understand it. Jamie's never tardy. He's been a great employee, apart from not reporting the break-in." She rearranged the box of fluffy toys on the counter, then bent and straightened a bag of dog food.

"I'm sorry to hear about your troubles, Sofia." Heather resisted the urge to whip out her notepad again. She'd already filled another one.

"Yeah, and that's not all I have on my plate. Several of my birds have vanished overnight. All the local kinds. I don't understand it. But this time, nothing's broken."

"Have you reported this yet?" Heather asked.

"No, I was just about to when you came in." Sofia braced her palms on the counter. "This would all be a lot easier if Jamie had decided to show up."

"I was going to ask you a few questions regarding the case, but perhaps they can wait until a time when you're not slammed," Heather said.

Sofia smiled at her. "Thank you. I appreciate that. I really do have a lot to do. Clean the tanks, the snake cages. Today was supposed to be Jamie's turn." Sofia slipped out from behind the counter again and walked toward the aisle. "Do you need anything else?"

"No, that's all. Thanks a lot, Sofia," Heather replied. She tapped her fingers on the top of the counter, and Amy appeared at her side. She jumped and turned to her bestie. "Gosh, you're getting good at popping out of places unexpected."

"We need to check on him," she said, in a low hiss. Like a balloon letting out air. "Now."

"Pardon me?"

"Jamie," Amy replied. "It doesn't make sense. I mean, why wouldn't he answer his phone? And where would he have gone to? I don't like this Heather. What if the killer has struck again?"

Heather eyed the bird cages, then reached up and massaged a spot in the middle of her forehead. "I highly doubt that, but I see your point."

Amy followed her gaze and gasped. "What if they used a bird this time?"

"Assuming the killer is some kind of fabled animal whisperer, of course."

"I'm serious," Amy said. "It all makes sense. Maybe Jamie knew too much and –"

Heather opened the front door of the pet store, and bell sounded again. She stepped out into the rain and Amy followed, hot on her heels.

"Ames, relax," Heather said. "My sleuthin' sense tells me there's another explanation for this. I agree, we need to check on Jamie, but I don't think there's any danger."

"You did bring your Taser, though, right? Just in case," Amy asked, and glanced up at the thunderclouds.

"Of course," Heather replied, and patted her handbag. It'd been a long time since she'd left the house without it. "Better to be safe than sorry."

Trouble always found Heather Shepherd, if she didn't find it first.

Chapter 15

"I don't know where he lives, Ames," Heather said. "I could call Ryan and ask him to check out Jamie's place, but if he's not answering his phone, he's probably not there."

"Or he's hurt," Amy replied, and grimaced. "I know I sound melodramatic."

"Just a tad, but you're right. We should check this out. I'll give Ryan a call."

They rounded the corner, and Heather whipped out her cell. She swiped her finger across the screen and clicked through to her contacts.

Amy grasped her forearm, and she nearly lost her grip on the phone.

"Amy," she hissed.

"Uh, Heather?" Her bestie whispered. "There's Jamie."

And there he was.

Jamie Purdue sat on the park bench, his head bowed, and his hands clasped together in front his knees. Two bird cages sat on the chair beside him, and two colorful birds hopped around inside and chirped to their heart's content.

"What's he up to?" Heather mused.

Amy took off toward the park and Heather followed, curiosity rumbling through her mind. Why would Jamie have stolen the birds from the pet store? And why on earth had he come to the park?

"Mr. Purdue," Heather said. The women strode up to him and came to a halt.

Jamie flinched and sat up straight. "Mrs. Shepherd, uh, Amy."

"Hi," Amy said, "what on earth are you doing?"

Jamie's lips peeled back and he half-grimaced, half-smiled. "I suppose it seems a little crazy. I, uh, I'm trying to free these birds."

"The birds from the pet store," Heather said, in a monotone.

"That's correct, yeah. I hate seeing them in the cages. Look, I can watch people walk out of the store with kittens and puppies and even fish, but the birds? It just feels wrong. They're meant to be free. They're meant to fly." Jamie cleared his throat and glanced down. "I quit my job to work in this pet store."

"So you could free the birds?" Heather asked.

Amy snorted, then blocked it with her fist. Even she thought it was a little cuckoo for cocoa puffs and she had her moments.

"No," Jamie said and chuckled. "That'd be ridiculous. I just wanted to spend time around animals. I wanted to be a vet actually, but I didn't make it in. So yeah, this was the closest I could get. The more time I spend with the animals, the more I realize how wrong this kind of thing is." He gestured to the cages beside him. "Sofia's obviously going to fire me when she finds out."

Heather tapped her fingertips on her tote and grasped her cell in her other hand. "Maybe she won't find out. Maybe she will."

"I don't want to cross her," Jamie grumbled. The noise matched his manly exterior to a tee, but the downturned lips didn't.

"Why's that?"

"She's got a major temper. Crazy bad." He rolled his eyes. "Now, I sound like I'm trying to make her out to be bad again. Look, she's a great lady. She's a good boss. Just don't get on her bad side." Jamie rose from his seat and tucked his hands into his pockets.

"What makes you say that?" Heather asked.

Jamie glanced at the street then down at the birds. "I guess I have a minute to talk about it," he said.

"Remember I told you about the fight between Sofia and JB Jones?"

"Yeah."

"Well, it was a bit more heated than I made out. She got real angry with him. She hit him over the head with a bag of dog food," Jamie said. He stifled a giggled.

Amy didn't bother. She laughed out loud.

"Dog food," Heather said.

"Yeah. She called him a dog too and a whole host of other things in Spanish," Jamie replied. "Couldn't understand most of them, but they weren't good."

"Then what happened?"

"Nothing," Jamie replied, and shrugged his shoulders. "I think JB was in a state of shock after that. He just kinda wandered off, muttering under his breath." Jamie made two fingers and walked them in mid-air.

"Why didn't you tell me this before?" Heather asked.

"I didn't want it to seem like Sofia killed him. She didn't. I'm pretty sure she has an alibi and everything," Jamie replied.

That was true. Sofia did have an alibi. But receipts could be faked. She could've reached out to several close friends and asked them to cover for her.

No, that would create too many weak links, and killers didn't like weak links in their chain of subterfuge.

Except this killer had been sloppy.

"What size shoe do you wear Jamie?" Heather asked.

He looked down at his feet and frowned. "Uh, that's kind of a weird question. I'm size eleven. You want my social security number, next?"

"You crack me up," Amy said and laughed again.

"No, I think that will be all," Heather replied. The guy was fine. Just a bit strange. Or maybe releasing birds back into the wild was a noble thing to do. It all depended on the perspective.

"Good," Jamie said. "Because I've gotta help out some friends." He turned back to the cages, then bent and unhooked their little metal meshed doors. He tapped the backs of the wire cage on the left, then whistled.

Three birds flew out and fluttered off toward the trees.

He did the same with the next cage, and the rest of the chirpy buddies twittered off into the morning.

Amy looped her arm through Heather's and smiled. "Would you look at that," she said.

"They're free." Jamie shut the cages, then stacked one on top of the other. "I'd better get back to work and tell Sofia what I've done, so she can fire me."

"Stay safe, Mr. Purdue," Heather said.

The man gathered a cage under each arm and walked off toward the street, his back straight as a rod and his shoulders relaxed.

Heather turned and directed Amy in the opposite direction. "Time to get back to work," she said.

"Suddenly, I wish I was one of those birds."

Chapter 16

Donut Delights bustled on any given afternoon, but Friday's were by far the busiest. People wanted their sweet treats before the start of the weekend, or maybe it was to celebrate the start of the weekend.

The rush hour had just ended, at least.

Heather handed out another coffee and a Donut Delights box. "Enjoy your Iced Pumpkin Donut, sir. Have a great afternoon."

"Thanks a lot," the businessman replied. His phone trilled in his pocket, and he balanced his coffee and box in one hand and whipped it out. "Hello? Peterson. Yeah, yeah, I've just arrived."

He turned and wandered to a table, then plopped his suitcase down.

"These darn foreigners invadin' our town," Amy said, and made a fist. "They're rootin' tootin' stealin' our jobs."

"Don't ever do that again," Heather said and laughed.

Amy stuck out her tongue. "The quality of my jokes has gone downhill this week. We have been busy, though, to be fair."

"To be fair," Heather said and sighed. She lowered her aching body into one of the stools behind the counter, then stretched out her legs. "Boy, it has been one heck of a week."

"You can say that again." Amy held up her palm to forestall Heather. "But don't. And it's not over yet."

"Yeah, I still have to figure out who actually slipped the snake into the poacher's apartment."

"That honestly sounds like a movie," Amy replied. She plonked down in the seat beside Heather's, then whipped out her smartphone and fiddled with it. "What does your gut tell you about the case?"

"My gut has been wrong before, so I'll reserve judgment until I have all the facts."

Amy wiggled her nose, gaze focused on the screen of her phone. "But it sounds to me like you already have all the facts."

"If that were the case, this mystery would've been solved already." Heather gave a wan smile. She couldn't muster the energy for a better one. She'd expended it all on the case and running around town, searching for the answers.

"So, let's go over it again."

Heather glanced around the store, but every customer had a

full mug or plate, and Emily had the waitressing job under control. No one would hear them amidst the chatter and joy.

"Our killer had small feet, or wanted to frame someone with small feet," Heather said.

"All right, what else?" Amy asked, and tapped on her screen again.

"Are you playing Candy Crush, right now?"

"No, Cookie Jam. Far superior game in my opinion," Ames replied. "You were saying."

"As if we don't get enough sweets in our everyday lives," Heather said, then cleared her throat. She raised a finger. "Right, as I was saying. The killer opened the netting and let the snake through."

"Which means the killer had to know how to handle a snake," Amy replied.

"That's correct. Coral snakes are dangerous. They'd have to have some experience with handling snakes," Heather said and massaged a sore spot on her neck. "Only two of our suspects have any knowledge when it comes to that. Sofia, who owns the store, and Jamie."

"But Jamie's shoe size doesn't match," Amy replied, and made another connection on her game.

"C'est Bon!" The game announced.

"Right, but he could've squished —"

"I dunno about that, Heather. I'm being biased here. I just highly doubt the man who frees birds in the park would squish his size eleven feet into size seven lady's shoes," Amy said. "Besides, he's a military man."

"Ex-military man," Heather replied. She stopped massaging her neck and dropped her hand into her lap. "Then we're out of options. Sofia has her rock solid, potentially fake alibi. Jamie probably wasn't as experienced handling snakes, and the shoe doesn't fit."

"So he can't wear it," Amy said.

Heather tilted her head to one side. "Huh, I can almost hear the drumroll and cymbal crash for that one."

"You're mean." Ames swatted her with one hand then returned to her game. "You know what this means, right?"

"What?"

"That your next suspect, or lead is a person who could handle snakes. I only know of one place in the entire town that does that."

"Hillside Snake Rescue," Heather hissed. "Of course! Why didn't I think of it before?"

Amy exited her game and opened her Google search bar. She typed in Hillside Snake Rescue, then searched. "Ah, instant results. Got to love technology."

Heather scooched closer. "What does it say?"

"Uh, just a disclaimer about what they do. Rescuing snakes. Snake removal. Reintegration into the wild. They have a charity page, too."

"What's that?" Heather asked and tapped on a tab on the screen.

"Volunteers, new and old," Amy said, out loud. She scrolled down the page and clicked her tongue. "Nobody I recognize. I guess you could phone the place and ask –"

"Stop!" Heather called out. "Go back up. Scroll up, for heaven's sakes."

"All right, all right, keep your donut on."

"That doesn't even make sense." Heather leaned closer to the screen and hummed The Sound of Silence under her breath. "There! That's the killer."

Amy stared at the picture. "Volunteered between the years of 2000 to 2004." She looked up and met Heather's gaze. "Penelope Walsh."

Puzzle pieces clicked together in Heather's mind. Penelope Walsh the activist with a penchant for shooting. She could handle snakes efficiently. Her prints had been on the outside of the tank.

She'd checked out the snake before stealing. All they had to do was match the shoe size to the shoes, and it was done.

"Heather?" Amy asked. "Are you okay?"

"Yeah, I just have to call Ryan and ask him to meet me here," she said.

"You're going to go with him?"

"Yeah, I need to understand what happened better," Heather replied. She smooshed her phone out of her pocket, then unlocked it and clicked through to Ryan's contact number for the second time that day.

"I think it's pretty clear what lady. That cat lady strikes back," Amy said. "Oh boy. I need to get a joke book or something."

"Look after the store for me until I come back?" Heather asked.

"Don't I always?"

"If you call eating the stock looking after it," she replied. She didn't mean it, of course, and Amy knew that.

Heather strode between the tables in Donut Delights and stripped off her apron. Finally, she'd understand why this had happened and why Penelope had been so messy about cleaning up after herself.

Heather pressed the phone to her ear.

Chapter 17

Heather and Ryan stood side-by-side in front of Mrs. Walsh's door and exchanged a single glance.

Ryan couldn't be nervous. He'd done this kind of thing hundreds of times.

Heather swallowed her butterflies whole, then raised her fist and knocked on the dark wood. "Mrs. Walsh? It's Heather Shepherd."

"Coming dear," the old lady called out from the inside. "Out the way, kitty." Her muffled whispered to her cats made Heather's insides twist.

Why had this kind old lady risked everything to kill the poacher?

The lock scraped back, and the door opened a second later. Penelope's drawn face appeared in the crack. "Oh hello –" She cut off and stared at Ryan's uniform. "Officer? May I help you?"

"Mrs. Walsh, I'm Detective Shepherd. We need to have a talk," he said. He didn't have to move an inch. His words came with an authoritative presence.

"Of course," Penelope said. She opened the door all the way, then stepped back a pace. "Please, come in."

Helpful, as always. Surely, she had to realize why they'd come. Heather inhaled and stepped into Penelope's home.

The elderly woman shuffled through to the kitchen, then gestured to the coffee pot. "Would you like something to drink?"

"No, thank you," Heather said.

Ryan shook his head. "Please, take a seat, Mrs. Walsh."

Penelope hesitated, then stumbled to one of the chairs and lowered herself into it. "All right," she replied.

"Do you know why we're here, Penelope?" Heather asked, softly. She sat down opposite the woman, but Ryan stood. He placed his palms on the back of Heather's chair and leaned on it.

"I – I have some idea. Is it about the poacher?" Penelope asked.

"It is about the poacher," Ryan replied. "Mrs. Walsh we have evidence which has led us to believe that you not only broke into the Sunny Hill Pet Store and stole a coral snake but further used that snake to murder Jimmy Bob Jones."

Penelope sat back and sucked in deep breaths. Her face screwed up into an expression of agony, then relaxed again. "I did it," she said, immediately.

Heather contained her shock at the easy admission. "Why?" She asked.

"I didn't want to endanger the coral snake. I felt terrible afterward. I was about to knock on the front door and warn the man, but then I heard him yell and bang into something and –" Penny cut off and shook her head. "I knew it was too late. Is the snake all right?"

"Uh, yes, the snake is all right," Heather replied. "But you realize the gravity of the situation, don't you, Mrs. Walsh?"

"I guess. I mean, it's not like I outright murdered him. I just put a snake in his apartment. It's not like I can be charged for anything, right?"

Ryan exhaled behind her, and his breath brushed the top of Heather's head. "I'm afraid your information is incorrect, Mrs. Walsh. By placing the snake in his home, with intent to kill, you are responsible for Mr. Jones' death. It's third-degree murder."

Penny's eyes went wide as donut holes. She looked from Heather to Ryan and back again. "No, that can't be true. I – I just wanted him to go away. I – he threatened my cats!" Penelope yelled.

"Please, calm down, Mrs. Walsh," Heather said. That was why the evidence had been left all over the place. Penny hadn't cared about being found out because she'd believed it wouldn't matter either way.

"He threatened my cats," the old woman repeated.

"Please, explain," Heather replied.

"I spotted him, as I told you, while I was walking my dog, Pebbles," Penelope said. "I yelled at him, and he yelled back. He said he knew where I stayed and that the Labrador was too muddy to sell, but my cats would do just fine."

"Oh wow," Heather said, and her lips twisted in disgust. "Did you report the incident?"

"No, of course not." Penny shook her head, and her eyes filled with tears. "Then I saw him a while later, and he yelled at the lady at the pet store. I got so angry. I usually go to the range and take out my frustrations, but this was the last straw."

"You went to the pet store," Heather said.

"Yeah, and I looked around, and I saw that darling coral snake and things just clicked into place in my mind. He had to die. And what a perfect way to go. Killed by the very animals, he hunted and displayed," Penny said, and her bottom lip quivered. She balled her hands into fists. "I'm glad he's gone."

A lot of people and animals were glad the man was gone, but that was no excuse.

"I'm sorry, Mrs. Walsh, but what you did is illegal," Heather said. "And deplorable."

"Don't you tell me what's deplorable, young lady," Penny replied, and wiggled her finger in mid-air. "I've lived longer, and I know far more than you. That poacher decimated our local wildlife. He needed to die."

Nausea drifted through Heather's stomach. She couldn't argue with that opinion because it would never change Penelope Walsh's mind.

To her, the choice had been obvious. She believed she'd done the right thing, the legal thing.

"My husband would've done the same, you know, if he'd been around. And he'd have chased you both out of my house," Penelope said, in a low growl. "He wouldn't stand for terrible police work or tomfoolery!"

Ryan stepped into view and unhooked his cuffs from his belt loop. "I'm afraid you're going to have to come with me now, Mrs. Walsh."

"Never!" She yelled. "You'll never take me alive." Penelope dashed toward the rifle on the wall.

Heather launched herself out of her seat and dove in front of the woman's path.

Penelope pulled up short and glared at her. "Get out of my way," she said and narrowed her eyes to slits. Tears still hovered there, in the corners.

"I'm sorry, Mrs. Walsh," Heather said, then nodded to her husband.

She despised the next part.

Chapter 18

"Thanksgiving festival," Lilly sang, and gobbled up the last of her pumpkin pie off her paper plate. "I love this. It's the best."

"I can't believe it," Amy replied. "It's not even Thanksgiving yet, and already they've put up a whole festival and games."

"Oh dear," Eva said and patted Amy on the arm. "Don't complain. Just enjoy the lovely weather and the treats."

Heather laughed and rested her head on Ryan's shoulder. They strode through the crowds and toward a distant stall.

"There it is!" Lilly yelled. Dave barked at her ankles and wagged his tail. Lilly plopped her paper plate into a trash can then darted on ahead, with her doggy companion hot on her heels.

"Oh my," Eva said. "She's difficult to keep up with these days. Legs are getting longer by the second."

"She's going to be taller than you, Ames," Heather said.

Amy threw back her head and laughed. "As if that's difficult."

The fall afternoon brought a gentle breeze, not too nippy for a change, and the skies were blue as a duck's egg. No clouds, no rain, almost the perfect weather for fussy Amy.

Heather's bestie shivered and dragged her coat closed.

Almost.

They group halted in front of the Donut Delights stall. Ken and Maricela waved from their spots behind the wooden construction. "We're almost sold out," Ken said. "The Iced Pumpkin Donuts are a total hit."

Heather's jaw dropped. They'd made dozens of the treats for the festival. Surely, it couldn't be true. Oh, well, she could always head back and whip another couple batches. "I'll run back to the store and –"

"No ways, boss," Maricela said. "All under control." She gave her a thumbs up. "Angelica and Emily go back to the store. They make the donuts now."

"Awesome," Heather said.

Lilly grinned, but her face fell a second later. "Wait, that means there are no donuts for Dave and me?"

"Sorry, no," Ken said. "But we'll have new stock soon."

Amy's expression mirrored the eleven-year old's.

"Look at the two of you," Eva said and flapped her hands. "You both ate your body weight in pumpkin pie and caramel apples. You can't possibly have room for more."

"Eva, you underestimate them, greatly. Dave too." Heather smiled at her best friend and the disheartened Lilly.

"Oh well," Lilly said, "I guess we'll have to do something else, Dave. They probably have games here."

Ryan squeezed Heather tight, then walked to Lilly. "Come on, you two. I'll take you to the games section."

They wandered off together. Lilly slipped her hands into Ryan's, looked up at him and proceeded to talk his ear off. He tilted his head toward her and listened, anyway.

Heather sighed and clasped her hands to her chest. This had been a good year so far. The best, actually, thanks to her friends, her family, and her store.

"Well, well, well, what do we have here?" A woman's voice sounded right behind her.

"Not again," Amy groaned.

Heather turned on the spot and instantly regretted.

Kate Laverne stood directly in front of the Donut Delights stall, her arms folded across her chest, and her foot tap-tap-tapped on the grass of the field.

"Oh dear," Eva muttered and scooted over to Amy's side of the argument.

"Kate," Heather said. "To what do I owe the distinct displeasure of your company?"

Laverne's upper lip twitched then settled. "You broke my business, woman. You owe me money, if not more."

"How do you figure that?" Heather asked. "If you can't compete in an already competitive market, then don't blame me for your losses."

"Oh, I'll compete, all right," Kate said and stepped up real close. "I'll compete. You'll regret what you just said."

"Is there a point to his one-man show?" Heather asked, and glanced up at the sky. She half-expected thunder clouds to roll in and lightning to flash through the gray. "I'd prefer to enjoy my Sunday afternoon, thank you."

"Oh wow," Kate said. "You haven't heard yet, have you?"

"Heard what?" Heather asked.

Kate threw back her head and laughed at the sky. Several

passersby gave her odd looks, then hurried off.

"Okay then. I'll be on my way," Heather said and made to turn.

"Hillside's annual baking competition is next week," Kate said.

Heather froze and glared at her. She'd totally forgotten about that. Usually, she competed, but this year had been so very busy, she wasn't sure the store would have the time to put in an entry.

"You're not gonna bow out, are you?" Kate asked. "Because I'll be there."

"Shouldn't you be back in New York, by now?" Heather checked her nails, then met Amy's gaze. Her bestie gave her a thumbs up for moral support.

"I'm not leaving. Not until I've taken your name and dragged it through the mud," Kate whispered.

"What was that?" Eva asked, loudly.

"She said she wants to drag Heather's name through the mud," Amy yelled back.

"How rude," Eva replied. "What horrible woman."

Kate's cheeks reddened, but she didn't back down. "So, what's the verdict, Shepherd? Are you in?"

Heather pursed her lips. She glanced at the Donut Delights stall and her two assistants, who stared open-mouthed.

She turned back to Kate and flashed her a confident smile. "I'm in."

THE END

A letter from the Author

To each and every one of my Amazing readers: *I hope you enjoyed this story as much as I enjoyed writing it. Let me know what you think by leaving a review!*
I'll be releasing another installment in two weeks so to stay in the loop (and to get free books and other fancy stuff) Join my Book club.

Stay Curious,

Susan Gillard

www.ingramcontent.com/pod-product-compliance
Lightning Source LLC
La Vergne TN
LVHW012142090325
805543LV00030B/631